Enid Blyton's
Twilight Tales

PURNELL

Text copyright © Darrell Waters Limited 1976, 1989
Illustrations copyright © 1976 Purnell & Sons
Illustrations copyright © 1989 Macdonald & Co (Publishers) Ltd

First published 1976 by Purnell Books
Reprinted 1989 by Purnell Books, a Division of Macdonald & Co (Publishers) Ltd

Macdonald & Co (Publishers) Ltd,
66-73 Shoe Lane, London EC4P 4AB

a member of Maxwell Pergamon Publishing Corporation plc

ISBN 0-361-03265-X
Printed and bound in Great Britain by Purnell Book Production, Paulton.
A member of BPCC plc

THE CHINA RABBIT

On the nursery mantelpiece sat a little china rabbit. It was a dear little thing, with perky ears, a little white bobtail, and two shining black eyes. It was not a toy, but an ornament, and the two children, Anna and Fred, liked it very much. But Nurse would not let them play with it in case they broke it.

"You leave it on the mantelpiece and let it look nice there," she said. "It's such a dear little brown rabbit, just exactly like a real one, but much smaller."

So the china rabbit lived on the mantelpiece and was very happy. It watched all that went on out of its shining black eyes. It saw Anna and Fred having their dinner. It saw Anna drop a piece of her pudding on the floor. It heard Nurse scold her. It saw Fred put too big a piece of cake in his mouth and choke dreadfully. Nurse banged him hard on the back and the cake shot out on the floor.

"Very bad manners," said Nurse crossly, and got the brush and pan. Oh, the china rabbit saw most exciting things, I can tell you.

It saw Fred being stood in the corner for smacking Anna. It saw Anna cutting her pretty hair with the scissors, and, dear me, the china rabbit quite trembled to think what Nurse would say to that! Nurse was so upset that she fetched Mother upstairs to the nursery. Dear, dear, dear, the things the china rabbit had seen!

It saw the toys come alive at night and play happily on the floor. How the

4

china rabbit longed to join them! But it wasn't a toy, so it couldn't. It just sat on the mantelpiece and looked and looked. Sometimes it laughed out loud, because the Teddy Bear was very funny. He put on the dolls' bonnets, and he rode on the clockwork mouse, and sometimes he fell off on purpose and rolled over and over on the floor, knocking down all the watching skittles as he went.

"Do it again!" the little china rabbit would cry. "Do it again!"

The toys were fond of the rabbit. The sailor doll often climbed right up to the mantelpiece to talk to him. The rabbit would listen and listen. But he never left the mantelpiece.

Now, one day a little black imp came into the nursery. He came from the mouse-hole, and all the toys stared at him in alarm, for he really was very black, very ugly, and very unkind.

He was quick and nimble, and he skipped about everywhere, pulling the dolls' noses, tweaking the toy cat's fine whiskers, tugging at the lamb's tail, and smacking the yellow duck's beak.

Then he saw the pretty little talking-doll hiding away in a corner, for she was very frightened of the black imp. The imp stared at her in surprise. He had never seen anyone quite so pretty and dainty. He ran over to her and took her hand.

"Come and live with me in my mouse-hole," he cried.

But the talking-doll said: "No, no, no!" and ran to the golly for help. Just then the cock crew—it was dawn. The imp had to go, but before he went he shouted: "I'll be back tomorrow. I'll fetch you tomorrow, talking-doll."

The toys were most upset. The next night they hid the baby doll, and where do you suppose they hid her? They hid her behind the big clock on the mantelpiece. It was a very good place. The china rabbit was pleased. He had always liked the pretty little talking-doll. It was nice to have her so close to him.

The golliwog came up to the mantelpiece too, to take care of her. He sat beside the china rabbit and stroked his ears, telling him all kinds of news.

And then suddenly the black imp popped out of the mouse-hole again. "Here I am!" he cried gleefully, and twisted his black tail about as if he were a cat. "Where's that pretty little doll? She is to come with me!"

Nobody answered. The imp was soon in a rage, for he guessed that she had been hidden. He ran to the brick-box and looked there, flinging out all the bricks. He ran to Nurse's work-basket and looked there, throwing out the needles and cottons. He ran to the box of puzzles and looked there—and you should have seen the nursery floor, quite covered with bits of puzzles by the time that black imp had finished with the box!

Now, he would never have found the little talking-doll if she hadn't peeped out from behind the clock to see what was going on. As she popped her pretty golden head out, the imp looked up and saw her. "There she is, there she is!" he cried. "I'll soon have her!"

He ran to the chair by the fireplace and began to climb up it. The golliwog by the china rabbit stood up and clenched his fists.

"Throw something at the imp, throw something at the imp!" cried the Teddy Bear from the hearthrug. The golly looked about for something to throw. There were three pennies on the mantelpiece. He would throw those. He picked one up. Whizz! It flew through the air, but the imp ducked and it missed him. The golly threw another. That missed the imp too, and so did the third penny. The imp climbed steadily up. He would be on the mantelpiece in a moment.

There was a marble on the mantelpiece, too, left there by Fred. Golly picked that up. Whizz! It flew through the air and hit the imp on the foot. He gave a yell of rage and shook his fist at the golly.

"Go on; throw something else!" yelled the toys below. "He's nearly there."

"There's nothing else to throw," shouted back poor Golly. "The clock's too heavy, and so is the money-box."

"Throw *me*, throw *me*!" cried the china rabbit, suddenly. "Quick, Golly, pick me up and throw *me*! I'll knock him down all right. I'll save the talking-doll."

"But you may break," said the golly.

"Never mind, never mind, just throw me! Oh, quickly, before it's too late!" shouted the rabbit.

So the golly picked up the little china rabbit and hurled him as hard as he could at the black imp, who was just about to climb on to the mantelpiece.

The rabbit flew straight for the imp. Crash! It hit him on the head. The imp fell to the ground and lay still. The rabbit fell to the ground too, but—oh, dear!— he smashed into a hundred tiny bits. Wasn't it dreadful? You couldn't tell which bit of him was ear or tail or nose or back—he was all in teeny-weeny scraps on the floor.

The toys were full of alarm. Poor, poor little rabbit! Whatever could they do for him? They picked up all his bits, and put them into a dish from the dolls' house. Then they looked at the imp. He lay in a faint with a great big bump on his head.

The bear fetched some string and tied him up tightly. Then he got a cup of cold water and dashed it over the imp's face. He opened his eyes and tried to get up.

"Oh, no, you don't!" said the golly, giving him a good punch to make him lie down. "You are nicely caught, imp. You will not be set free in a hurry, I can tell you."

"What was it hit me?" asked the imp, looking round.

"It was the poor china rabbit," said the Teddy Bear, wiping his eyes with his bow. "He was smashed to bits."

"Serve him right," said the imp.

"Oh!" said the golly fiercely. "If you talk like that, imp, we'll drop you out of the window and see how *you* like being smashed to bits."

"Oh, no, no, no!" cried the imp, in fright. "Don't do that to me. Perhaps I can mend the rabbit for you, I have some magic glue here."

He sat up and they took it from his pocket. It was in a queer long tube. The golly untied the imp's hands, but his legs were still tied.

"If you can mend the rabbit, begin right away," said the golly. "Here are the bits. Put them together and get him right again. You shall not go free till you've finished."

The imp stared at the hundreds of tiny bits in dismay. Then he set to work. He worked all that night—and the next—and the next and soon the toys saw the shape of the china rabbit coming again. The imp stuck each tiny bit together in its right place. During the daytime the toys kept him tied up inside the box of the Jack-in-the-Box, and only let him out at night. It was a real punishment for that imp, I can tell you!

At last the china rabbit was quite mended again, though there was one bit over which didn't seem to go anywhere at all. All the glue in the tube was finished. The toys gathered round the rabbit in delight.

"Welcome back, brave little china rabbit," they said. "Can you talk to us?"

The china rabbit found his tongue. It felt rather gluey, but he managed to talk all right.

"How's the talking-doll?" he asked.

"Quite well, thank you!" she said, and gave him a big hug. "Oh, rabbit, it's nice to have you again! It was dreadful when you were all in bits. You shall go back on the mantelpiece again tonight."

So up he went, carried carefully by the golly, and there he stood once more, beaming down at everyone. As for the imp, he slipped away down the mouse-hole when no one was looking, but as everyone knew he would be much too frightened to come back again they took no notice.

Fred and Anna were so pleased to see the china rabbit again. They had been very puzzled when he disappeared. They looked at him carefully and saw that he was covered with tiny, tiny cracks.

"Look, Nurse," said Fred; "he looks almost as if he had been broken into bits and mended again."

"Don't be silly," said Nurse. "Who would mend him if he broke into tiny bits, I'd like to know?"

The china rabbit stared and stared at Nurse and longed to tell her who had mended him. But he didn't say a word. He still sits there, as pretty as ever, just beside the clock. You'll see him if ever you go to play with Fred and Anna. Don't forget to look for the tiny, tiny cracks all over him, will you?

THE BEAR AND THE DUCK

Once upon a time there were two toys, a bear and a duck. They lived on the top shelf in the toy-shop, and they had been there for a whole year. Fancy that! A whole year!

They were very unhappy about it. It was dreadful not to be sold. They got dustier and dustier, and at last they almost gave up hope of ever having a little boy or girl to own them.

You see, by some mistake, the duck had a bear's growl and the bear had a duck's quack. It was most upsetting. Whenever the bear was squeezed in his middle, he said "Quack! " very loudly indeed—and whenever the duck was squeezed she said "Grrr-rrrrrr!"

The shopkeeper had tried to sell them, but she couldn't, and that was why she had put them away on the top shelf.

One day a little girl came into the shop with her mother. She was seven years old that day, and she had come to spend the money that her granny had given her for her birthday.

"I want a duck and a bear," she said. Then she pointed up to the shelf. "Oh,

10

look!" she said. "There are two there, and they are just the size I want."

The shopkeeper took them down from the top shelf—and, oh, how excited the duck and bear felt when they thought they really might be sold to this nice little girl!

"Do they say anything?" she asked.

"Well," said the shopkeeper, "it's rather funny. The bear quacks like a duck, and the duck growls like a bear. A mistake was made, and it is impossible to put it right."

The little girl pressed the bear and he made a quack loudly. Then she pressed the duck and it had to growl—grrrr-rrrrrrr!

"Oh," said the little girl, disappointed, "what a pity! I don't like a bear to quack and a duck to growl. It's all wrong. I'm afraid I don't want them."

THE BEAR AND THE DUCK

The bear and the duck could have cried. The little girl looked at them again, and they looked so sad that she felt sorry for them.

"I'll see if I can get a bear that growls properly and a duck that quacks in the right way somewhere else," she said. "But if I can't—well, I might come back and buy these two."

"Very well," said the shopkeeper, and she put the two toys back on the top shelf again. They watched the little girl take her mother's hand and go out of the shop. They felt most unhappy. To think they could have been sold and gone to the same nursery to live with a nice little girl like that.

That night the bear spoke to the duck. "Quack!" he said. "Duck, listen to me. It's quite time we did something to help ourselves."

"Grrr-rrrrrr!" said the duck. "I agree with you. But what can we do?"

"Quack," said the bear, thinking hard. "We will go to the Little Wise Woman

on the Hill, and ask for her help. Maybe she can do something for us."

"Grrr-rrrrr, goodness me!" said the duck in surprise. "Dare we?"

"Quack! Certainly!" said the bear, and he jumped down from the shelf. The duck followed and they went to the window, which was open at the bottom. Out they went, and walked over the wet grass. The duck had to waddle rather than walk, so they couldn't go very fast.

At last they came to the hill where the Little Wise Woman lived. Her cottage was at the top, and the two toys could see that it was lighted up gaily.

"Perhaps she has a party tonight," said the duck, out of breath; "I do hope she hasn't."

But she had—and just as the two toys got to the cottage the guests began to go. Out went Dame Big-Feet, the witch, on her broomstick, and with her flew her black cat. Out went Mrs. Twinkle, the fat woman who sold balloons all day and made spells at night. After her went Mister Poker-Man, who was as tall and as thin as a poker, and last of all went little Roll-around, who was as round as a ball, and rolled down the hill instead of walking.

"They have nearly gone," whispered the duck to the bear. "Let's wait outside till the cottage is empty."

So they waited in a corner until all the goodbyes were said, and then they crept out. They peered in at the window, and to their great surprise they saw the Little Wise Woman sitting on a chair, groaning and crying.

"Oh my, oh my!" she said. "I'm so tired, and there's all this mess to clear up before I go to bed."

The bear and the duck couldn't bear to see her so unhappy. They went in at the door, and spoke to the Little Wise Woman.

"We will clear up everything for you," said the bear. "Don't worry. The duck will help you to get to bed, and will make you a nice cup of tea, and give you a hot-water bottle; and I will sweep up the mess, clear the table, and wash up."

The Little Wise Woman was so surprised that she didn't know what to say.

THE BEAR AND THE DUCK

"Why, you're from the toyshop," she said at last. "However did you manage to get here tonight?"

"Never mind," said the bear, determined not to talk about his own troubles now. "You just get to bed, Little Wise Woman, and go to sleep. We'll do everything else."

"Grrr-rrrr!" growled the duck kindly, much to the Little Wise Woman's surprise.

"Quack!" said the bear, and surprised her still more. Then she remembered that her friend, the toyshop woman, had told her about a bear who quacked and a duck

who growled, and she thought these must be the two queer toys. How kind they were to come and look after her like this, just when she had so much to do!

The duck took her into the bedroom and helped her to undress. She made a cup of nice hot tea, and gave her a hot-water bottle. Then she tucked her into bed, turned out the light, and left her to go to sleep. The duck was not going to worry the Little Wise Woman about her own troubles now. Not she!

The bear was very busy, too. He cleared all the dirty dishes off the table, and washed them up. He put them neatly away, and swept the floor. Then he put the cakes into their tins and the biscuits into their jars, and put the lids on.

He was very hungry, but of course he didn't dream of taking even half a biscuit. He knew it would be wrong, and he was a very good little bear.

Just as he had finished his work the duck came creeping out of the bedroom.

"She's almost asleep," she said in a whisper. "We'd better go."

"I'm not quite asleep," said the Little Wise Woman, in a drowsy voice. "Before you go, look in my kitchen drawer. You will find two boxes of pills there. Bear, take a yellow pill. Duck, take a blue one. You won't be sorry you came to help me tonight."

"Thank you," said the bear, astonished.

He knew that the Little Wise Woman had many marvellous spells, and he wondered what would happen when he and the duck swallowed the pills. Perhaps he would grow beautiful whiskers, and maybe the duck would grow a wonderful tail.

He took a yellow pill, and the duck swallowed a blue one. Then they carefully shut the kitchen drawer, called goodnight to the Little Wise Woman and went out into the night.

They were very tired when they got back to the toyshop. They climbed up to their shelf, leaned back against the wall, and fell fast asleep at once.

They didn't wake up until the sun was shining into the shop. The doorbell woke them with a jump and they sat up. They saw the same little girl who had come to the shop the day before. She looked up at their shelf and pointed to them.

"May I see that duck and bear again?" she asked. "I couldn't find any just their size yesterday, so I've come back to see them again."

The shopkeeper lifted them down. The little girl looked at them.

"It *is* a pity the duck growls and the bear quacks," she said.

She pressed the duck in the middle—and to everyone's enormous surprise the duck said "Quack!" very loudly indeed. The most surprised of all was the duck herself. She had never in her life said "Quack," and it felt very funny.

Then the little girl squeezed the bear, and to his joy and astonishment he growled!

"Grrr-rrrrrr!" he went. Just like that!

"What a funny thing," said the little girl. "Yesterday they did just the opposite. Have you had them mended?"

"No," said the shopkeeper, just as surprised as the little girl. "They've not been taken down from their shelf since you went out of the shop. I can't think what has happened."

THE BEAR AND THE DUCK

The little girl pressed the bear and the duck again. "Grrr-rrrrrr!" growled the bear. "Quack!" said the duck. They were both most delighted. So that was what the pills of the Little Wise Woman had done—made their voices perfectly all right. How lovely!

"Well, I will buy them now," said the little girl. "There's nothing wrong with them at all, and they are just what I wanted. I think the bear is lovely and the duck is a dear. I shall love them very much."

How pleased the two toys were when they heard that! When the shopkeeper popped them into a box, they hugged one another hard—so hard that the duck had to say "Quack!" and the bear had to say "Grrr-rrrrrr!"

"Listen to that!" said the little girl, laughing. "They're saying that they're glad to come home with me."

The duck and the bear are very happy indeed now, and you should just hear the duck say "Quack!" and the bear say "Grrr-rrrrrr!" whenever the little girl plays with them. They have quite the loudest voices in the nursery.

GETTING UP

I've slept all night through—at last I'm awake,
And out of the window a peep I will take.
What's the day like—is it cloudy or fine?
Is the rain going to pour, or the sun going to shine?

I feel full of beans, though I've not eaten *one*;
I'm ready for shouting and jumping for fun,
I'm hungry for breakfast—oh, what do I smell?
Fried egg and bacon—and sausage as well!

Where are the soap and the towel and the brush,
Where are my vest and my shorts? What a rush!
My garters have gone—I do think it's queer
The way that my garters and socks disappear.

I've found them—hurrah!—now I *must* brush my hair,
And fold my pyjamas and put them just there!
I do feel so happy, I'm singing, I'm humming;
There's somebody calling—YES, MUMMY, I'M COMING!

CHINKY TAKES A PARCEL

Chinky was doing his shopping in the pixie market. It was full today, and there were a great many people to talk to. Chinky was a chatterbox, so he loved talking.

His market-bag was full. He had no more money to spend, and it was getting near his dinner-time. "I really must go home," said Chinky, and he picked up his bag.

"Hi," called Sally Simple, "did you say you were going home? Well, just deliver this parcel to Mrs. Flip's, next door to you, will you? It's for her party this afternoon."

"Certainly," said Chinky, and he took the square box, which felt very cold indeed.

"You are sure you are going straight home?" asked Sally Simple anxiously. "I don't want you to take the parcel unless you are really off home now."

"I'm going this very minute," said Chinky. "Goodbye!"

He set off home—but he hadn't gone far before he met Dame Giggle, and she had a funny story to tell him. He listened and laughed, and then he thought of a *much* funnier story to tell Dame Giggle.

So it was quite ten minutes before he set off home again—and then who should he meet but Old Man Grumble, who stopped him and shook hands. Chinky hadn't seen Old Man Grumble for a long time, and he had a lot of news to tell him. He talked and he talked, and Old Man Grumble hadn't even time to get one grumble in!

"You *are* a chatterbox, Chinky," he said at last. "Goodbye! Perhaps you'll let me get a word in when next we meet."

Chinky set off again. The square cold parcel that he was carrying for Sally Simple seemed to have got very soft and squashy now. It was no longer cold, either. It was rather warm and sticky!

"Goodness! I wonder what's in this parcel?" thought Chinky, hugging it under his arm.

A little drop of yellow juice ran out of one corner and dripped down Chinky's leg. It was ice-cream in the parcel—a big yellow brick of it that Mrs. Flip had ordered for her party. She meant to put it into her freezing-machine when she got it, and then it would keep cold and icy till four o'clock.

Chinky went on his way humming. Some more ice-cream melted and ran down his leg. Chinky didn't know. He was nodding excitedly at little Fairy Long-wings, who was standing at her gate.

"Hallo, Long-wings!" called Chinky. "Glad to see you back. How did you enjoy your holiday?"

And, dear me, he stood talking at Long-wings's gate for ten minutes. Long-wings didn't tell him a word about her holiday, for Chinky was so busy chattering about himself and his garden and his shopping. And all the time the ice-cream dripped down his leg.

Well, when at last he arrived at Mrs. Flip's, the box was almost flat and empty. He handed it to Mrs. Flip, and she looked at it in dismay.

"My ice-cream for the party!" she cried. "It's all melted! Look at your clothes, Chinky—what a mess they are in! Well, really, you might have brought it to me at once! I suppose Sally Simple gave it to you, thinking that you were coming straight home!"

"Well, so I did!" said Chinky indignantly. "I came *straight* home, as straight as could be!"

"I don't believe you," said Mrs. Flip. "I know you, Chinky—the worst chatter-box in town! Oh, yes! You met Mr. So-and-so, and you talked to him for ages—and you saw Mrs. This-and-that, and you chattered for ten minutes—and you came across Dame Such-and-such, and you had a good long talk! And all the time my ice-cream was melting. Take it! I don't want it now—it's just an empty box."

She threw it at Chinky and it hit him on the nose. He was very angry. He shook his fist at Mrs. Flip and shouted: "I shan't come to your party now! I just shan't come!"

"Well, don't, then!" said Mrs. Flip, and she went inside and banged her door. Chinky banged his.

Soon there was the sound of the ringing of a tricycle bell, and along came the ice-cream man. Mrs. Flip heard him and out she ran. She bought the biggest ice-cream brick he had, all pink and yellow. She popped it into her freezing-machine for the party that afternoon.

And when Chinky looked out of his window at half-past four, he saw everyone busy eating ice-creams in Mrs. Flip's garden, as happy as could be.

"Why didn't I go straight home as I said I would? Why did I say I wouldn't go to the party? I talk too much, that's what's the matter with me!" said poor Chinky.

He was quite right, wasn't he? You would think he had learned his lesson, wouldn't you? But he hadn't. At first, he was quite good, but it wasn't long before he was chattering and gossiping as much as ever. Chatterboxes can't be stopped—easily . . . you try stopping one, and see!

OLD MOTHER WRINKLE

Old Mother Wrinkle was a strange old dame. She lived in an oak-tree, which had a small door so closely fitted into its trunk that nobody but Dame Wrinkle could open it. It was opened many times a day by the old dame, for always there seemed to be somebody knocking at her door.

The little folk came to ask her to take away their wrinkles. Fairies never get old as we do—but sometimes, if they are worried about anything, they frown or sulk, and then lines and wrinkles grow in their faces. Frown at yourself in the glass and see the ugly wrinkles you get!

Mother Wrinkle could always take away any wrinkle, no matter how deep it was. She would take a fairy into her round tree-room, sit her down in a chair and look at her closely.

"Ho!" she might say. "You've been feeling cross this week. There's a very nasty wrinkle right in the middle of your forehead. Sit still, please!"

Then she would rub a curious-smelling ointment on the fairy's forehead to

25

loosen the wrinkle. Then she would take up a very fine knife and carefully scrape the wrinkle off. She would powder the fairy's forehead and tell her to go.

"But don't you frown any more," she would call after her. "It's a pity to spoil your pretty face."

Now, Mother Wrinkle had taken wrinkles away for two hundred years, and the inside of her room was getting quite crowded with the wrinkles. She didn't like to throw them away, for she was a careful old dame. She packed them into boxes and piled them one on top of the other.

But soon the boxes reached the top of her room—really, there must be a million wrinkles packed into them. What in the world could Mother Wrinkle do with them?

Now, the fairies did not pay her for taking away their wrinkles. Sometimes they brought her a little pot of honey, sometimes a new shawl made of dandelion fluff—but the old dame hardly ever had any money, and she needed some badly.

"I want a new table," she said, looking at her old worn one. "I would love a rocking-chair to rock myself in when I am tired. And how I would like a pair of soft slippers for my old feet."

She told Sammy, the rabbit, about it one day when he came to bid her good morning. He nodded his long-eared head. "Yes," he said, "you do want some new things, Mother Wrinkle. Well, why don't you sell those boxes of wrinkles and get a little money?"

"Sell the wrinkles?" cried the old dame. "Why, I'd love to—but who would buy them? Nobody! If people want to get rid of wrinkles they certainly wouldn't pay money to buy some. That's a silly idea, Sammy Rabbit!"

The rabbit lolloped off, thinking hard. He liked the old woman. She was always generous and kind. He wished he could help her. He talked to the pixies about it. He spoke to the frogs. He told the hedgehog. He spoke to the bluebell fairy—and last of all he met the little primrose fairy, and told her.

She listened carefully, and then she thought hard. She had been very worried for the last fifty years because the primroses,

26

which were her special care, had been dreadfully spoilt by the rain. Whenever it rained the wet clung to the leaves, ran down to the centre of the plant, and spoilt the pretty yellow flowers. It was such a nuisance. She had been so worried about it that Mother Wrinkle had had to scrape away about twenty wrinkles from her pretty forehead.

But now she had an idea. Suppose she took the wrinkles that the old dame had got in her boxes! Suppose she pressed them into the primrose leaves! Suppose she made them *so* wrinkled that when the rain came the wrinkles acted like little river-beds and drained the water off at once, so that it didn't soak the leaves and spoil the flowers!

"What a good idea that would be!" thought the primrose fairy joyfully. "I'll try it."

So she went to Mother Wrinkle and bought one of the boxes of wrinkles. She took them to her primrose dell and set to work. The primrose leaves, in those days, were as smooth and as thin

as beech leaves—but when the fairy began to press the wrinkles into the leaves, what a difference it made!

One by one the leaves started to change. Instead of looking smooth they looked rough and wrinkled. In the middle of her work the rain came down, and to the fairy's delight the wrinkles acted just as she had hoped—the rain ran into them and trickled to the ground in tiny rivulets!

"Good!" said the fairy, in delight. "Now listen, primrose plants! You must grow your leaves in a rosette and point them all outwards and downwards. Then, when the rain comes, your wrinkles will let it all run away on the outside—and your flowers will be kept dry and unspoilt."

Little by little the fairy gave wrinkles to every primrose plant, and they grew well, till the woods were yellow with the flowers in spring. Mother Wrinkle was delighted to sell the old wrinkles. She bought herself a new table, a fine rocking-chair, and two pairs of soft slippers.

And now you must do something to find out if this strange little story is true. Hunt for the primrose plant—and look at the leaves. You will see the wrinkles there, as sure as can be—delicate and fine—but quite enough to let the rain run away without spoiling the pale and lovely flowers.

THE INQUISITIVE HEDGEHOG

There was once a most inquisitive hedgehog, who liked to know everybody else's business. He used to shuffle round the ditches, listening to all that the toad said to the frog, and trying to find out where the squirrel had hidden his winter nuts.

The pixies who lived in the hedgerows were most annoyed with him, for he was always trying to find out their secrets, and, as you know, pixies have many magic secrets which no one but themselves must know. Whenever they met together to talk they had to be sure to look under the dead leaves or behind the ivy to see if Prickles the hedgehog was hiding there ready to listen.

Now, one day a wizard called Tonks came to visit the pixie Lightfoot, who lived in a small house in the bank of the hedgerow. This house had a little door overhung with a curtain of green moss, so that no one could see it when passing by.

Inside the door was a cosy room, set with little tables, chairs, and couches, for Lightfoot often had parties and needed plenty of furniture. There was a small fireplace at one end, and on it Lightfoot boiled his kettle and fried his bacon and eggs.

Tonks was to come and have a very important talk with Lightfoot and the other pixies about the party that was to be given in honour of the Fairy Princess's birthday the next winter. Prickles overheard the toad telling the little brown mouse, and he longed to know what day the party was to be, and if the creatures of the hedgerows were to be invited as well as the fairy folk.

But nobody could tell him, for nobody knew. "Nothing is decided yet," said

the toad; "and even when it is I don't suppose *we* shall know until the invitations are sent, Prickles. You must just be patient."

"Yes, but, you see, I want to go and visit my grandmother, who lives far away on the hillside," said Prickles. "And if I choose a week when the party is held it would be most unfortunate."

"Well, we shan't miss you very much," said the toad, going under his stone. He was not at all fond of the inquisitive hedgehog.

Prickles wondered and wondered how he could get to know what the pixies would say when Tonks the wizard came to talk with them. And at last he thought of an idea. "If I creep into Lightfoot's house just before the pixies and the wizard go there to meet, and cover myself with a cloth, I shall look like a sofa or a big stool, and no one will notice me. Then I can lie quietly under my cloth and hear everything," he thought to himself. "What a good idea!"

THE INQUISITIVE HEDGEHOG

So he borrowed a red shawl from the old brownie woman who lived in the hazel-copse, and stuffed it into a hole in the bank, where an old wasps' nest had once been. Then he waited impatiently for the evening to come when Tonks was to see the hedgerow pixies.

At last it came. Prickles took his shawl out of the hole and went to where the green moss-curtain hung over Lightfoot's little door. As he crouched there, looking like a brown clod of earth, the door opened, and Lightfoot ran out. He was going to fetch some cakes. He left his door open, and Prickles quickly went inside.

The room was neatly arranged with chairs and stools in a circle. Prickles pushed them about and made room for himself. He threw the red shawl over his prickly back and crouched down, looking like a couch without a back, or a great stool. He was pleased. Now he could hear everything.

Very soon Lightfoot came back. He was humming a little tune, as he put out the cakes neatly on a dish and set the kettle on the fire to boil water for some tea.

Presently there was a knocking at the door. Lightfoot opened it. In came the pixies from the hedgerow, chattering and laughing.

"Find seats for yourselves," said Lightfoot. "I'm just making the tea. I've some cakes, too, if you like to help yourselves."

"We'll wait till old Wizard Tonks comes," said the pixies. They sat down on the chairs and began to talk. Prickles listened hard with both his ears, hoping to hear a few secrets.

Rat-tat-tat! Someone knocked loudly on the door. It was Tonks the wizard. Lightfoot ran to open it, and bowed the old wizard into the cosy room.

"Good evening, everyone," said Tonks. He was a round, fat wizard, with white hair and a white beard that was so long he had to keep it tied up in a big knot or he would have tripped over it.

"Good evening!" cried the pixies, and they all stood up, for the wizard was a wise old fellow, and everyone respected him.

"Well!" said Tonks, taking off his long black cloak. "We have come to discuss a most important matter together—the party for the Fairy Princess this winter."

"Won't you have a nice cup of hot tea before you begin the meeting?" asked Lightfoot, coming up with a big cup of steaming-hot tea. "Sit down and make yourself comfortable, Tonks."

Tonks looked round for a seat. He was fat and rather heavy, so he chose the biggest seat he could see, which, as you will guess, was Prickles the hedgehog under his red shawl!

Tonks sat down heavily, holding his cup of tea in his right hand and a cake in his left.

But no sooner had he sat down than he shot up again in a fearful hurry, shouting, "Oh! Ooooh! Ow! Pins and needles! What is it? Ooooooh!"

He was so scared at sitting down on the prickly hedgehog that he upset his hot tea all over the two pixies who were sitting next to him. His cake flew up into the air and hit Lightfoot on the head when it came down! Dear, dear, what a commotion there was, to be sure!

"What's the matter, what's the matter?" everyone cried.

"Ooooooh!" said the poor wizard, rubbing himself hard, for the hedgehog was very, very prickly, and all the prickles had pricked Tonks when he sat down so hard.

"Oooooooh!" said the two pixies who had been scalded by the tea.

"Ooooh!" said Lightfoot, wondering what had hit him.

"How dare you put pins and needles on the seat left for me?" roared Tonks suddenly, shaking his fist in Lightfoot's face. "How dare you, I say?"

"Whatever do you mean?" said Lightfoot, most astonished. "Don't talk to me like that, please, Tonks. I don't like it. And, anyway, what do *you* mean by throwing your nice hot tea over my friends?"

Prickles began to think he was going to get into trouble. So he began to move quietly towards the door, but a pixie saw him and shrieked with fright.

"Look at that sofa! It's walking! Oh, look at it! It's gone magic!"

All the pixies looked at what they thought was a sofa walking towards the door. Tonks looked too.

"Why, that's the sofa I sat down on!" he cried. "It was as prickly as could be! Catch it! Quick! Catch it!"

Prickles was very frightened. He ran towards the door, and just as he reached it a pixie pulled at the red shawl he had thrown over himself.

"Oh! It's Prickles, the inquisitive hedgehog!" cried Lightfoot angrily. "He came here and hid himself to hear our secrets. No wonder poor Tonks thought he was sitting on pins and needles! Catch him!"

But Prickles was safely out of the door. He banged it behind him and scurried off through the ditch. He made his way through the stinging-nettles, and ran to a hole in the bank that he knew very well. A big stone covered the entrance and a fern grew over the stone. He would hide there!

Tonks, Lightfoot, and all the other pixies raced after him. They did not like stinging-nettles, so they went round them, and by the time they had got to the other side Prickles was nowhere to be seen.

"Find him, find him!" raged Tonks. "I'll teach him to prick me! Yes, I will! I'll make him eat a dinner of needles cooked in hot tea! I'll pull out all his prickles! I'll—I'll—I'll——"

Prickles heard all that Tonks was saying, and he trembled in his hole. He was safe there, and the stone and fern hid him well. He did hope that no one would find him.

No one did. The pixies hunted for a long time, and then gave it up.

"He must have gone to his grandmother on the hillside," said Lightfoot. "Let's go back."

"Now listen!" said Tonks fiercely. "You keep a look-out for that rascal of a hedgehog all the winter. As soon as he shows his nose bring him to me! I'll keep a fine meal of cooked needles for him! I'll be going away to Dreamland in the spring-time, so find him before that."

THE INQUISITIVE HEDGEHOG

"Yes, Tonks," said the pixies. "We are always about this hedgerow, so we are sure to see him. Anyway, he will come to the party; we'll catch him then."

Prickles heard, and how he trembled when he heard of the cooked needles!

"I shan't get out of this hole until Tonks goes to Dreamland," he decided.

So all that winter Prickles kept in his little hole. He did not go out to catch beetles or slugs, but just curled himself up and slept soundly. He only awoke one night when he heard a noise of laughing and chattering—and when he poked his nose out he found that it was the party that was being given in honour of the Princess's birthday! Poor Prickles! He didn't dare to go to it and he saw the rabbit, the hare, the squirrel, and the little brown mouse all hopping and running along to have a good time, but he had to keep close to his hole.

It really served him right, didn't it? And, do you know, it's a strange thing, but ever since that winter hedgehogs have always slept through the cold days! Perhaps they are still afraid of Tonks! I shouldn't be surprised.

UNCLE NAT'S CHRISTMAS-TREE

It was three days before Christmas, and Mary and Peter were very excited.

"Mummy says she's going to buy us a Christmas-tree!" Mary told her Uncle Nat. "It will be a nice big one, and it will cost a terrible lot of money."

"Oh, I'll bring you in a tree for Christmas," said Uncle Nat. "A nice, shapely spruce fir, which will fit well into a pot."

"Well, I think we'd rather have a Christmas-tree, thank you, Uncle Nat," said Mary earnestly; "one we can dress up and clip candles to. I like Christmas-trees, with their funny, prickly leaves. I wouldn't like any other tree."

"But, my dear child, you will be able to dress up the spruce fir-tree as much as you like," said Uncle Nat, beginning to laugh. "If I bring you one, it will save your mother a lot of money, and you can spend it on ornaments and candles and tinsel instead."

Peter suddenly twinkled at Uncle Nat. "Yes, Uncle Nat," he said, "you bring us in a nice spruce fir, please, and we'll spend our money on ornaments for it. It's very kind of you."

Uncle Nat laughed again and went out. Mary was cross. She frowned at Peter.

"Silly! We've always had a proper Christmas-tree for Christmas, always! I don't want Uncle Nat's silly spruce fir, whatever it is. It won't look a bit nice. I want a proper Christmas-tree out of a shop!"

"Well, when you see Uncle Nat's tree, you'll think differently," said Peter, and went out to see what his uncle was doing.

"I shan't! I shan't!" Mary shouted after him, quite losing her temper for once. "I won't dress the silly tree. I won't hang anything on it at all."

She kept her word. When she heard Uncle Nat and Peter dragging in a big tub in which a tree was planted, she ran upstairs. "You can dress it by yourself!" she said to Peter.

Well, Uncle Nat and Peter did dress it. They hung tinsel strands on the spruce fir, they draped it with bits of cotton-wool to look like snow, they hung shining ornaments on it, and they clipped many coloured candles here and there.

"It looks really lovely!" said Peter. "Let's call Mary to see it."

So they did, and she came downstairs, feeling a little ashamed of herself. When she saw the tree, she clapped her hands in delight.

"Oh! You've got a real Christmas-tree, after all! How lovely! Oh, it's the most beautiful one we've ever had. Did Mummy buy it?"

"No, silly; it's the spruce fir that Uncle Nat brought in from his own garden," cried Peter. "Didn't you know that all Christmas-trees are young spruce trees, stupid? Well, they are!"

"Oh, dear!" said Mary, and went very red. "I'm sorry, Uncle Nat. I deserve to be punished for being so silly."

"And so you shall be," said Uncle Nat, with a twinkle in his eye. "I shall make you point out every single Christmas-tree next time we go to the woods—and if you get them all right, you shall have, for a reward, the fairy doll I've put at the top of the tree!"

Well—I hope Mary gets the reward, don't you?

NOT GETTING UP

This morning I'm really a sleepyhead,
I can't get out of my nice warm bed;
It felt so cold when I put out my hand
That I took it back into Blanket-land!

I'll try a toe—it's gone out to see
If it's warm enough for the rest of me!
Goodness, it's freezing—come back again!
Well, I can't get up this morning, it's plain!

I shall pull the blankets right over my head;
I shan't get up, I shall sleep instead.
No school for me for a day or two,
I'll hibernate, as the animals do.

Oh dear—I've remembered, there's no school today;
It's Saturday morning—I've all day to play!
I must get out of bed, I just HATE to be in it;
Where are my things? I CAN'T WASTE A MINUTE!

THE PARTY IN THE HOLLOW TREE

John was very good at climbing trees. He could climb every tree in his garden except one little apple-tree that was too small to bear his weight.

"I'm tired of climbing trees in the garden," John said to his sister Polly one day. "I'd like to climb some big trees out in the wood. Would you like to come with me? You can't climb them, but you can watch me."

"All right," said Polly. She wasn't at all good at climbing, but she loved to hear John say what he could see from the top of the trees he climbed. So off they went one sunny afternoon into the wood.

First John climbed this tree, then that tree. He told Polly that from the top of the first tree he could see Farmer Giles' cows far away in the meadow, standing up to their knees in the stream to cool themselves. Polly wished she could see them too, but she knew she would never be able to climb to the top branch as John did.

From the top of the next tree John could see Mrs. Jones hanging out the washing in her garden down the hill. That was a very long way to see.

And from the top of the next tree—but wait a minute, that was the funny old hollow tree that was so surprising inside!

John climbed up it, not knowing that it was hollow, for it was so big and sturdy-looking. He got halfway up and then happened to look down. And he saw that the tree was quite hollow inside, so hollow that there seemed to be a little room there, round and dark.

And in that little room there was a small table with four little chairs set round it! On the table was a yellow cloth with a border, and set on the cloth was a meal! There were four blue plates, four blue cups and saucers with little silver spoons, a plate of brown bread and butter, a pot of jam, a plate of chocolate cakes, and a teapot and jug of milk. John was so astonished that he nearly fell down the tree!

"What can you see from the top of that tree, John?" asked Polly, peering upwards.

"I say, Polly! What do you think? This tree is hollow inside and I can see such a funny thing!"

"What?" asked Polly.

"I can see a table laid for tea, and four little chairs set round it," said John.

"I don't believe you," said Polly. "You're just making it up."

"I'm *not!*" cried John. "I'm not! It's perfectly true. What a pity you can't come up and see it! Oh, Polly, I wonder who's going to go to the tea-party inside this tree. I'd love to see."

"I don't believe you one bit," said Polly. "I'm sure you're just pretending, to make me sorry I can't climb as well as you can."

"No, I'm not, I tell you," said John. "Oh, Polly, do believe me. We've often wanted to see fairies, and now, if only you'll be quiet, I believe we shall be able to see some. Hide under a bush, there's a good girl, and watch to see who comes to this tree. I expect there's a secret door to it somewhere."

So Polly went to hide, and John sat as still as a mouse up in the tree, peeping downwards to where the tea-table was set in the hollow below.

Suddenly, from out of a tiny trap-door behind one of the chairs, a small gnome appeared. John could hardly believe his eyes. Then another one came, and then two more. They all took their places at the little table, and began to eat their tea.

As they ate they talked. John could hear quite plainly what they said. They were talking about a dance that the Fairy Queen was giving that very night.

"It's to be under the gorse bush that grows highest up the hill," said one gnome, eating a piece of bread-and-butter very quickly.

THE PARTY IN THE HOLLOW TREE

"What time?" asked the gnome next to him, pouring out a cup of very strong tea.

"When the moon looks through the fir-trees yonder," said the first gnome. "Pass me a cake, please."

"Do you know, I feel as if humans were somewhere about," said the third gnome, solemnly.

"Yes, I feel a bit uncomfortable too," said the last one, drinking his tea rather noisily. "But there's nobody near us, I'm sure."

And at that very moment John's nose began to tickle dreadfully, and, oh, dear

me, he gave a most *enormous* sneeze! A-TISHOO! Then another—A-TISHOO!

The gnomes leapt up from the little table and gazed upwards through the branches. When they saw John they gave a shout of dismay, clapped their hands loudly together, and vanished completely. The table disappeared too, and all the chairs. There wasn't a thing to be seen!

John was so upset. He hoped the gnomes would come back, but they didn't. So he called Polly and told her all he had seen.

But Polly just *wouldn't* believe him! She thought he was making it all up again. John was quite angry with her, but it wasn't a bit of use. She hadn't seen the gnomes herself nor the tea-table, and she thought it was all make-believe.

"Well, I'm going to climb right down inside the hollow part, and see if I can find anything that the gnomes left," said John, crossly. "I never knew such a disbeliever as you, Polly."

So he carefully lowered himself down inside the tree and looked round. At first he could see nothing at all except cobwebs—and then he saw something shining white on the ground. He picked it up.

It was a square card, quite small, and on it was printed an invitation.

To the Hollow-Tree Gnomes.
Please Come to a Dance
On Full-Moon Night,
By Invitation of the Fairy Queen

"There!" cried John, in glee. "They've dropped their invitation-card. Now Polly will have to believe me!"

He climbed out of the tree and showed her the card. She really did believe his story then, and looked tremendously excited.

"Oh, John, I'm sorry I thought you were making it all up," she said. "Do you think—oh, do you think we might creep out tonight and hide somewhere to watch the dance?"

"Yes, we will!" said John, in great excitement. "Oh, Polly, what fun! We'll hide under the next gorse-bush to the highest one on the hill; then we shall see and hear beautifully."

I do wonder what they'll see, don't you? They're going tonight, and taking the gnomes' card with them, so that if they see the gnomes again they can return the card and ask whether they may join in the dance too.

I expect they will be allowed to—in fact, I'm sure they will—and I *do* wish you and I were going too!

The Fairy Queen's Dance at Full Moon

A SURPRISE FOR THE WAGTAILS

A pair of wagtails built their nest in some creeper that straggled over a roof. It was a nice nest, and soon it had four little eggs in it.

"Now, I must sit on them to keep them warm," said the hen wagtail. But first she flew off with her mate to catch some of the midges flying in the sunshine.

Whilst she was gone a big cuckoo saw the nest. Now, the cuckoo had made no nest, but she had to have one to put her egg in. So, whilst the wagtails were away, the cuckoo put her egg into their nest, and took out one of the eggs already there. Then she flew off, cuckooing loudly.

The wagtails came back. They didn't notice that one of the eggs was a little larger and not quite the same colour as the others. The hen wagtail sat down to keep them warm. She felt very happy. It is always nice for a bird to feel her warm eggs under her.

Two of the eggs hatched out. One little bird was bigger than the other. He was very bare and black and ugly. He couldn't bear to feel the two eggs near him,

44

nor could he bear to feel the other baby bird pressing against him. When the wagtails had left the nest for a little while, he managed to get one of the eggs on to his back, climbed up to the edge of the nest with it, and tipped it over! Out it went and smashed on the roof.

Then he sank down into the nest, tired out. But it wasn't long before he got the other egg on to his back and tipped that out too!

Then it was the turn of the baby bird. After a lot of struggling the tiny cuckoo got the baby wagtail on to his back, climbed slowly up to the edge of the nest, and tipped him out as well. He squeaked feebly, but no bird seemed to notice him.

Now the baby cuckoo was happy. He had the nest to himself. He settled down and waited for food.

The wagtails were surprised when they found that only one bird was in the nest. "But see how big he is!" they cried. "He seems to grow almost as we look at him. What a fine bird he will be! Finer and bigger than any other wagtail in the garden."

They fed him well. They were very proud of him. They called the other birds to see him. "Did you ever know a finer wagtail baby?" they said. "Isn't he magnificent?"

Soon the baby filled the nest. Then